Today's Cast Of Squirbles

Pip

Celeste

Percy

Salvador

Evangeline

Lunchbox

Newton

Murph

Dice

Today's Cast Of Squirbles

(continued)

← Estelle and Stanley Humpferdink

A VERY MERRY SQUIRBLEWEEN

Written & Illustrated by Kate Teves

Scan below for more Squirble® books + activities!

www.thesquirbles.com

A Very Merry Squirbleween. © Copyright 2022 by Kate and Christoph Teves. Printed in the United States of America. www.thesquirbles.com. Book layout designed by Kate Teves. The Squirbles are a registered trademark of Kate and Christoph Teves. All rights reserved. No part of this publication may be reproduced, distributed, or transmitted in any form or by any means, including photocopying, recording, or other electronic or mechanical methods, without the prior written permission of the publisher, except in the case of brief quotations embodied in critical reviews and certain other noncommercial uses permitted by copyright law. For information regarding permissions, contact us at: www.thesquirbles.com/contact

Special thanks to Christoph Teves, the less Humpferdinky of the two of us, for naming the Humpferdinks the Humpferdinks, and for providing excellent editorial suggestions throughout the project. Thank you to Patricia Merrow for her generous encouragement. And thank you to my parents—for everything.

for my parents

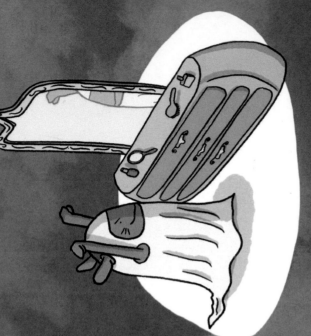

The sun was just setting
on a dark Squirbleween.
We posed, and we primped,
and we planned, and we preened.

Then we met up as one
and we marched in the streets
to peruse the whole town
for good tricks and good treats.

The goblins, the ghosts, and the trolls and the mummies got chocolates and lollies and suckers and gummies.

But when we arrived at this house at the bend,
we knew that our fun would now come to an end.

This is the house where the Humpferdinks dwell:
two grumpy old grouches who bicker and yell.

No matter the subject,
no matter the season,
they gripe and they grumble
without any reason.

But the worst day of all—
when they're at their most mean—
is that day of the year
that we call Squirbleween.

Maybe they're frightened,
or maybe they're jumpy,
or maybe they're just...

VERY DOWN IN THE DUMPIES.

There's only one time
when I've seen these two pleasant:
when they're snooping around
for their Christmassy presents.

On that holiday morning,
their lips turn up slightly,
and their eyes tend to glimmer
just a little more brightly.

When the holiday's over,
they go back to their funk,
and Humpfer they dink,
and Humpfer they dunk.

Well, we knocked on their door,
and we tried to look darling,
and we waited outside,
but heard nothing but snarling.

"Get out of our yard!"
they called out to us fast.
"No Humpferdink handouts—
it's just like years past!"

At last we gave up,
and we left with no meeting.

We moped to the road
without tricking or treating.

But just as we turned
to head home for the night,
a friend hatched a plan
that could make things all right.

"We won't get more candy,"
he explained with great care,
"but we'll bring Squirble joy
to that Humpferdink pair!"

Each of us now was assigned a new job...

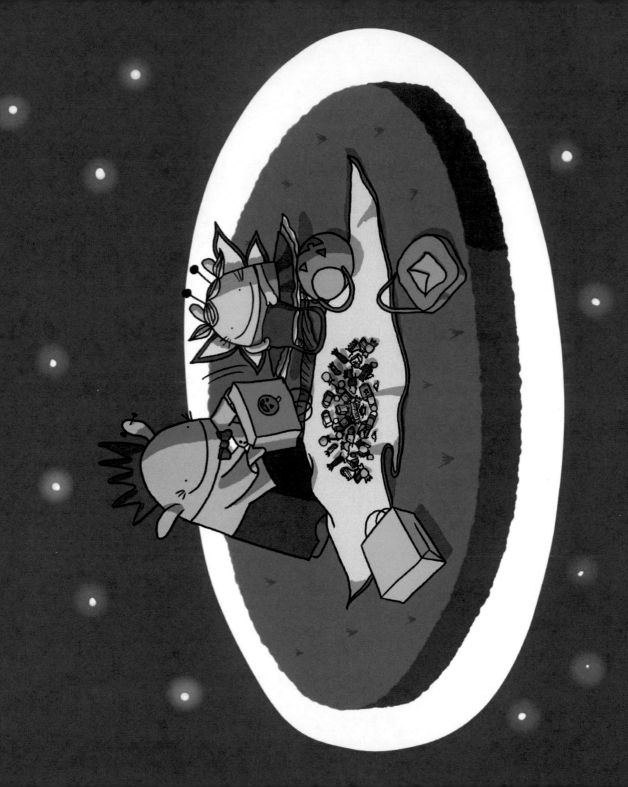

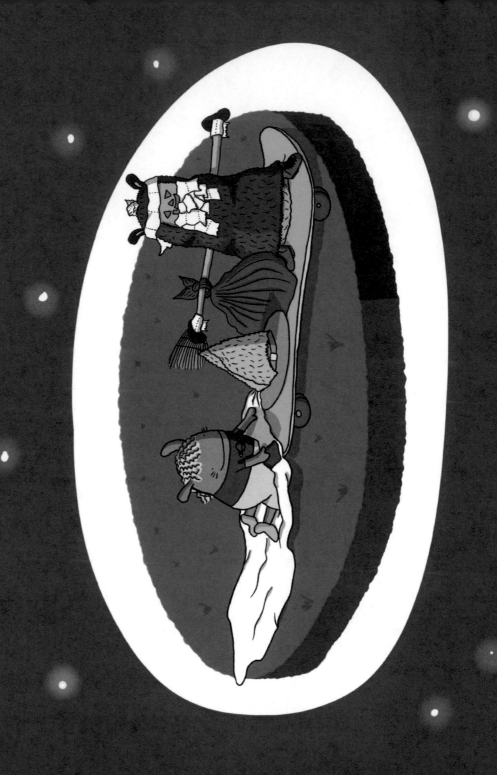

...and together we made a great thing-a-ma-bob!

At last we released it!
It flew without pause!
It sailed through the town
like a great Santa Claus!

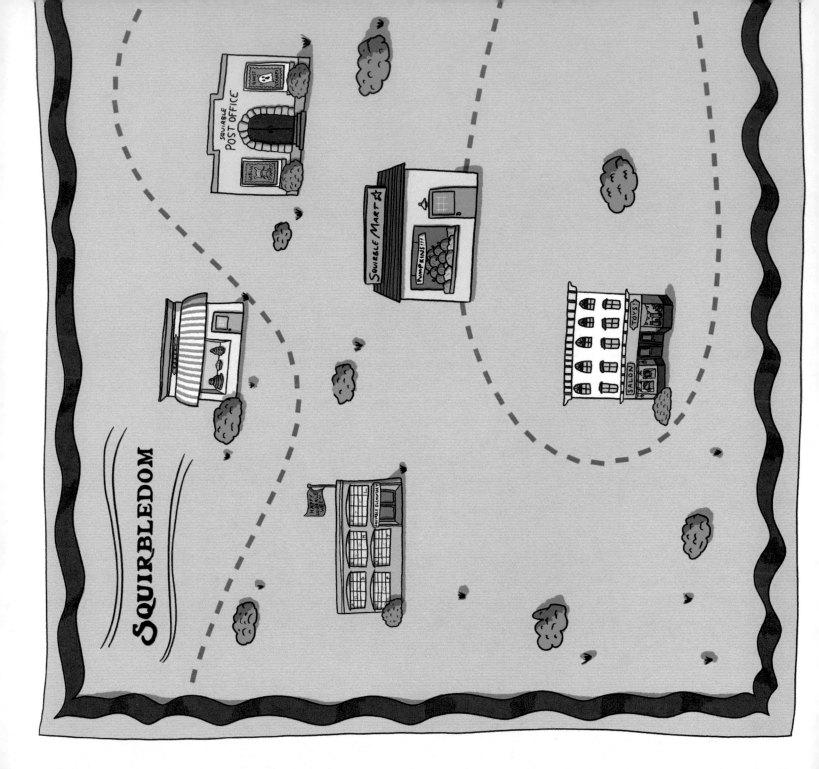

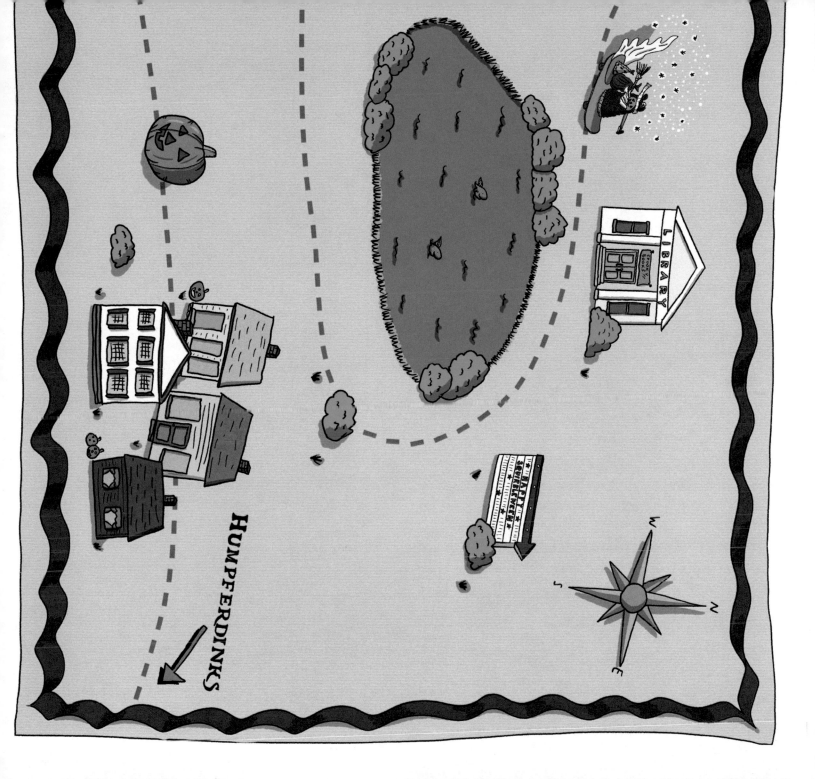

We watched as the Humpfs
now paraded with glee—
with stockings, a wreath,
and an elf, and a tree.

But just as our Santa
had reached its most dashing,
it slammed on a pothole
and found itself crashing!

We thought that the flop
would now shatter these two,
and they'd see that their Christmas
was very untrue.

Their joy would be finished
in just a few pinches!
They'd come after us
like two grumpy old grinches!

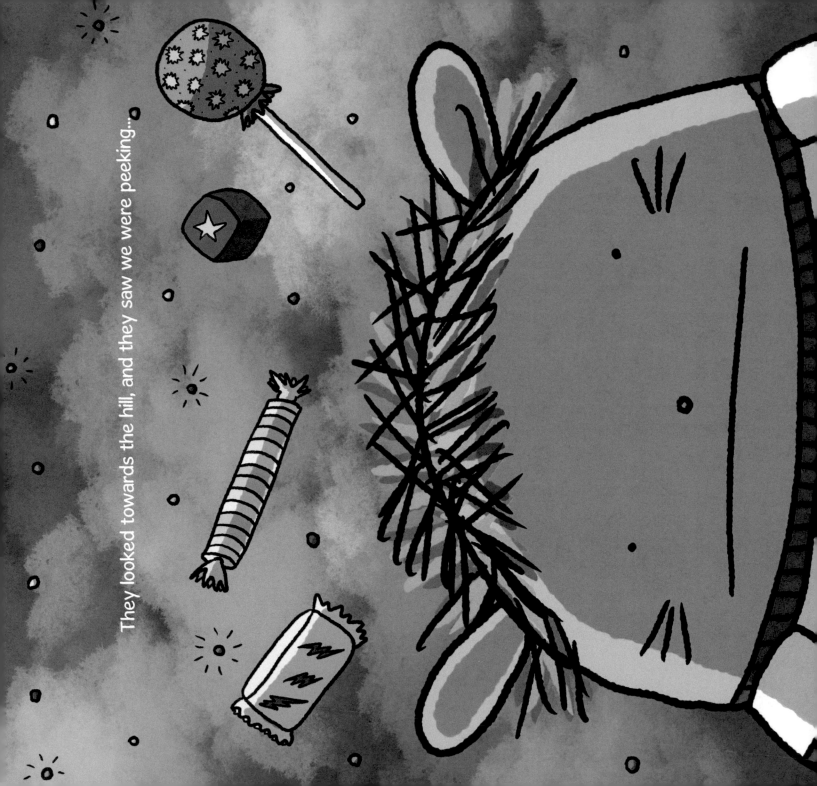

They looked towards the hill, and they saw we were peeking...

... and slowly they rose and approached without speaking.

They tossed us the candy! They sang, and they pranced!
They begged us to join in their feast and their dance!

"Oh, please eat these goodies!" they said of the bounty.
"Have all that you want! Have any amounty!
All of this time we've thought Squirbleween scary,
but now you have made it so wonderfully... MERRY!"

So you see:

Sometimes our neighbors
are tough little stinkers,
but really their hearts
are like old Humpferdink-ers';

They're just a wee trampled,
or worn out, or fading,
but try a bit harder—
they need some persuading!

Love,
Me (Percy!)

Made in the USA
Columbia, SC
15 October 2022

69076899R00031